# the CRiTTeR club

## Amy Is a Little Bit Chicken

by Callie Barkley ♥ illustrated by Tracy Bishop

**LITTLE SIMON**
New York London Toronto Sydney New Delhi

LITTLE SIMON

An imprint of Simon & Schuster Children's Publishing Division • 1230 Avenue of the Americas, New York, New York 10020 • First Little Simon paperback edition December 2015 • Copyright © 2015 by Simon & Schuster, Inc. • All rights reserved, including the right of reproduction in whole or in part in any form. LITTLE SIMON is a registered trademark of Simon & Schuster, Inc., and associated colophon is a trademark of Simon & Schuster, Inc. For information about special discounts for bulk purchases, please contact Simon & Schuster Special Sales at 1-866-506-1949 or business@simonandschuster.com. The Simon & Schuster Speakers Bureau can bring authors to your live event. For more information or to book an event contact the Simon & Schuster Speakers Bureau at 1-866-248-3049 or visit our website at www.simonspeakers.com. Designed by Laura Roode. The text of this book was set in ITC Stone Informal Std.
Manufactured in the United States of America 1115 FFG 10 9 8 7 6 5 4 3 2 1
Library of Congress Cataloging-in-Publication Data
Names: Barkley, Callie. | Bishop, Tracy, illustrator. Title: Amy is a little bit chicken / by Callie Barkley ; illustrated by Tracy Bishop. Description: First Little Simon paperback edition. | New York : Little Simon, 2015. | Series: The Critter Club ; #13 | Summary: "Amy has never liked being in the spotlight. When all her friends decide to form a team for the Santa Vista Quiz Bowl, Amy's not so sure. She knows she can answer the quiz questions . . . but can she do it in front of hundreds of people? Meanwhile, The Critter Club is caring for some chickens that need a home. As the Quiz Bowl approaches, Amy herself starts feeling just a little bit chicken!" Provided by publisher. Identifiers: LCCN 2015023879| ISBN 9781481451741 (paperback) | ISBN 9781481451758 (hc) | ISBN 9781481451765 (ebook) Subjects: | CYAC: School contests—Fiction. | Anxiety—Fiction. | Friendship—Fiction. | Chickens—Fiction. | Clubs—Fiction. | Animal shelters—Fiction. | BISAC: JUVENILE FICTION / Readers / Chapter Books. | JUVENILE FICTION / Animals / General. | JUVENILE FICTION / Social Issues / Friendship. Classification: LCC PZ7.B250585 An 2015 | DDC [Fic]—dc23 LC record available at http://lccn.loc.gov/2015023879

# Table of Contents

# Chapter 1

# Cluck, Cluck!

Amy swung the barn doors open. Sunlight and fresh air came in. Dust and dirt went out as Amy began sweeping the barn floor. It was a beautiful Sunday—cleanup day at The Critter Club.

Amy and her best friends, Marion, Liz, and Ellie, talked as they worked.

"My mom took me to the art museum yesterday," Liz said. She was wiping down the tables. "We saw some Chinese brush paintings. They were so beautiful!" Liz sighed.

"I want to learn how to paint like that!"

Amy smiled. Liz was always planning her next art adventure.

Ellie was emptying the garbage

can. "I spent yesterday making up a dance routine," she said. "Then I put on a show for my family!"

Ellie showed the girls some of the moves—ballet leaps, jazz taps, and hip-hop bounces. Liz, Marion, and Amy clapped. Ellie was such a fearless performer.

Marion told them about her

Saturday lunch with her grandparents. "After that, Coco and I had our horseback-riding lesson." Coco was Marion's horse. "We started working on jumping over ditches!"

*Wow!* Amy thought. She could not imagine flying through the air on a horse!

"I didn't do anything *that* exciting," Amy said. She explained that she'd checked out a brand-new mystery from the library. "Actually, that *was* pretty exciting. Then I started writing a story of my own. It's a fantasy story about a giant, evil—"

*Cluck, cluck, baaawk!* A hen came wandering into the barn. Two more followed right behind her.

"A giant, evil *chicken*?" Liz asked. Amy, Ellie, and Marion laughed.

The chickens had arrived the day before. They had been wandering

around downtown Santa Vista. They had even walked into the road, stopping traffic! No one knew where they'd come from. And no one knew what to do!

Then Ms. Sullivan happened to

pass by. She knew a place the chickens could stay while their owner
was found—The Critter Club!

Already the girls had learned
a lot about keeping chickens. For
starters, they needed a coop, or

henhouse. Luckily Ms. Sullivan's neighbors offered to help. Mr. Mack was a farmer and Mrs. Mack was a carpenter. Together, they made the perfect coop-building team.

The girls went outside to see how it was coming along. Behind the

barn, Mrs. Mack was hammering a shingle onto the coop roof.

"Wow! It's almost done!" Ellie exclaimed.

"We have a few more things to add inside," said Mrs. Mack.

Mr. Mack nodded. "Like the

nesting boxes where the hens can lay their eggs."

While Mrs. Mack finished the coop, Mr. Mack had a job for the girls: to help him make a chicken run. They used mesh fencing to enclose a large piece of the barnyard. "Now the chickens have a safe area to run around in," Mr. Mack said. "Let's try to get them inside of it."

That was easier said than done! Marion tried shooing the hens in. But they flapped their wings and went in the wrong direction.

Ellie tried singing to them: "Here, chicky, chicky, chicky." The hens didn't come.

Liz tried picking one up. The hen flapped and squawked loudly. Liz had to put her down.

Amy tried luring them with chicken feed. But when she tossed some toward them, the hens ran away from it.

"It seems like they're afraid of *everything*," Amy said to Mr. Mack.

He smiled. "Chickens sometimes are kind of . . . chicken."

# Chapter 2

# Fire Drill

Amy thought about the chickens as she walked into school the next morning. It was presentation day, and she was nervous.

The week before, everyone in class had made posters of an animal of their choice. It was hard for Amy to choose just *one* favorite animal. In the end, she chose the owl. There were so many cool facts about owls! Amy loved that part of the project.

But today everyone would present his or her poster. That meant standing up and talking *in front of the whole class.*

Inside Mrs. Sienna's room, Amy saw Marion, Ellie, and Liz by the coat hooks.

"Amy, you're here!" Marion said. "I wanted to tell all three of you at the same time. I have exciting news!"

Amy hung up her jacket and

backpack. Then she huddled up with her friends.

"So what is it?" Ellie asked. Marion opened her mouth to answer.

Just then, Mrs. Sienna called out, "Okay, class, take your seats! Time for Monday morning announcements. Then we'll begin the presentations!"

Amy groaned. Marion shrugged.

The girls split up and sat down at their desks.

Amy wondered what the big news could be. She was itching to know. But she was happy to have something to think about besides her nerves. She thought about the surprise while the first three

students presented their posters.

Then—too soon—Mrs. Sienna called Amy's name. It was her turn.

Amy carried her poster to the front of the room. She tried to read clearly and slowly as she pointed to each animal fact. But her hands were shaking. And she could feel her face blushing.

After what seemed like forever, she was done. The class clapped as Amy hurried back to her seat.

From the desk behind her, Ellie tapped Amy on the back. "That was so great!" Ellie whispered.

Amy shrugged. "It didn't feel great," she whispered back. "But it's over!"

She watched the rest of the class do their presentations. *How come they all look so confident?*

Liz was presenting her poster on chameleons. She seemed as calm as

ever talking about their cool color-changing ability.

Suddenly a loud noise filled the room. The whole class jumped. It was the fire-alarm siren!

"Fire drill!" Mrs. Sienna called. "Calmly push your chairs in and line up at the door."

# Chapter 3

# Marion's Exciting News

Mrs. Sienna's class filed down the hallway and out a back door. They walked to the edge of the playground. They lined up between the first graders and the third graders. Mrs. Sienna took attendance. Amy was in line in front of her friends.

Marion leaned forward and whispered her news. "I signed us

up as a team for the Santa Vista Quiz Bowl!"

Ellie and Liz heard and turned. Ellie clapped silently but excitedly. Liz gave a thumbs-up.

Amy looked back at Marion and smiled while mouthing the word "cool!" Amy loved trivia and quiz games.

But then all of a

sudden she felt a pang of dread.

*Wait. Is the Quiz Bowl that trivia contest they have at the huge theater? The one that* a lot *of people come to watch?*

Amy would have to wait until later to ask. Mrs. Sienna was walking up and down the line. She had her finger to her lips. They weren't supposed to talk during fire drills.

Finally at lunch, Amy and the girls had time to chat. Marion unpacked her lunch while she explained.

"I went with my dad to the grocery store yesterday," she said. "There was a woman there with

a Quiz Bowl sign-up sheet. It's for kids ages eight to fifteen."

Ellie beamed. "Good thing we're all eight already!" she said.

Marion nodded. "It's divided up by age. So we're in the second- and third-grade division!"

Marion pulled a folded-up paper from her pocket. "I copied this down from the Quiz Bowl website. It's a list of topics that the

questions might cover."

Amy's eyes lit up. *I bet I could do pretty well in literature,* she thought.

Liz leaned forward. "When is it? When is it?" she asked eagerly.

"Exactly three weeks from yesterday!" Marion exclaimed.

Amy breathed a little sigh of
relief. At least she had some time to
get used to the idea.

# Chapter 4

# Oops . . . Paint Fight!

After school Amy's mom dropped her off at The Critter Club. She and the girls had some fun but messy work to do. All of them had changed into old clothes.

The chickens were roaming happily in the chicken run. The coop was all done. It looked great.

Ms. Sullivan had found the

chickens' owner. He was a farmer who'd had the hens in the back of his truck. And they had escaped! But he was going out of town so he asked if The Critter Club could watch the hens until he returned.

In the meantime, Liz had decided the coop needed something more.

Color! So she had drawn up a color plan for it.

The girls had brought some left-over paint from home. They had yellow, white, red, and green.

Liz passed out brushes. Then they each took a paint bucket and started painting.

Marion brushed the red paint onto the roof. Liz was covering the walls with the green. Ellie brushed white on

the window trim. Next to her, Amy painted a shutter yellow—her favorite color.

Amy dipped her brush into her bucket, loading it with color. As she

raised it to the shutter, the brush flicked some paint drops. They landed on Ellie's arm.

Ellie gasped.

Amy looked over, realizing what

had happened. "Whoops!" she
cried. "Guess I had too much paint
on my brush. Sorry, Ellie!"

Ellie's shocked look turned into
a devilish smile. "Oh, yeah?" she
said. She dipped her paintbrush

in the white. She reached out and painted a stripe on Amy's arm.

"Hey!" Amy cried with a laugh. She aimed her brush at Ellie's shirt. Ellie ducked out of the way. The paintbrush landed on Liz's cheek instead.

Amy gasped. "Oops—again!"

"Ah!" Liz cried, her eyes wide in shock. She touched her now-yellow cheek. "Amy!"

"It was an accident!" Amy said.

Liz smiled. "I know." She dipped her brush into the green. "But this isn't!"

Defensively, Marion dipped her brush into the red. "Paint fight!" she cried.

Suddenly paint was flying everywhere. Amy put more yellow on her brush. She covered her face with one arm. With the other, she waved the brush to spray the yellow around.

43

She could feel paint drops hitting her arms and her hair! "Aaaaaaaah!" she shrieked between giggles.

Only a minute into the battle, Rufus came bounding over. "Woof!" he barked, and wagged his tail. He sprang and jumped around them, as if asking to play too.

"Stop!" Marion called. "Truce!"

The girls lowered their brushes. No one wanted to get paint all over Rufus. He'd need a doggie bath for sure. And getting Rufus in the tub wasn't easy!

Ms. Sullivan had followed Rufus outside. She walked up and stood over the girls, who had fallen to the ground, laughing.

"What a creative way to paint a chicken coop," Ms. Sullivan said.

The girls turned to look at the coop. It was splatter-painted all over in red, yellow, white, and green. That made the girls laugh even harder.

"I have to say," Liz said, "it looks pretty good!"

Amy, Ellie, and Marion agreed.

It was the most cheerful-looking chicken coop Amy had ever seen!

# Practice Makes Perfect

The girls told Ms. Sullivan all about the Quiz Bowl.

"That sounds wonderful!" she said. "I don't remember having those where I grew up. But I did win a spelling bee or two!" Ms. Sullivan got a faraway look in her eye. "I would study so hard beforehand. My mother quizzed me from the dictionary." Ms. Sullivan smiled at them. "So think about practicing. It helps!"

Amy thought that was a great idea. Maybe the more she prepared, the less nervous she would be!

"How about this," Amy said. "Let's each come up with five questions. Then tomorrow at lunch, we can quiz each other."

The others agreed. "Good plan, Amy!" Marion said.

That night after dinner, Amy tried to think of a good geography question. It came to her as she

cleared the table: *What is the capital of California?*

She knew that one. It was Sacramento. But it gave her the idea to sit down with her atlas. She scanned the U.S. map and reviewed all her state capitals.

United States of America

Later, while brushing her teeth, Amy thought about tricky spelling words. *What's that word I spelled wrong on my homework last week?* Envelope! *I always thought it was* onvelope.

Amy looked it up to make sure: E-N-V-E-L-O-P-E.

She thought up three more tough ones.

*Who was the first President of the*

*United States? George Washington!*
*What do all birds have that no*
*other animal does? Feathers!*
*How many planets*
*are in our solar*
*system? Eight!*

The next morning,
Amy couldn't wait until
lunchtime! Would her friends
know the answers to her questions?
Would she know theirs?

On the way into the cafeteria,
Amy passed two third graders. One
of them, a girl named Samantha,
stopped Amy.

"I saw your name on the Quiz Bowl sign-up sheet!" Samantha said. "Good luck!"

Amy smiled. She was about to say thanks, but before she could, the other girl, Danielle, added: "Yeah, good luck. The questions are *really hard.*"

The third graders walked off. Amy felt a knot in her stomach. She trudged to her lunch table. Liz, Ellie, and Marion were there. Amy told them what the girls had said.

Marion waved it off. "Don't worry about it," she said. "They were on the team that won our division last year. They entered this year too."

Ellie added, "Hmm. So we'll be competing

against them. They were *trying* to make you nervous."

"Well, it worked!" Amy said.

Amy tried to shake it off as she read her questions to her friends.

They got them all right—no problem!

Then Ellie read hers. "What's the name for a scientist who studies the weather?"

All Amy could think of was

"Weatherperson," but she knew that wasn't right.

"A meteorologist!" Liz called out confidently.

"Right!" said Ellie. "Okay. How many stars are on the American flag?"

Amy tapped her forehead. The answer was on the tip of her tongue. But Marion beat her to it. "Fifty!" The girls practiced for the rest of lunch. Between them, they knew all the answers!

But Amy had been keeping a tally in her head. She had only known a few of the answers. And *a few* weren't going to win the Quiz Bowl.

# Chapter 6

# Amy's Got a Frog in Her Throat

For the next three weeks, the girls brought new questions to lunch every day. They tested one another at The Critter Club when they went to feed the chickens. Amy asked her mother to quiz her at the dinner table.

Two days before the Quiz Bowl, Amy invited the girls for a

Friday-night sleepover. Amy's mom made them a big dinner of lasagna and salad. They took a box of question cards from a junior trivia game Amy had. They went through all of them while they ate.

Amy was getting more of the answers. But she was still nervous.

"They probably won't ask us any of these questions," she pointed out.

Her mom put a hand on Amy's shoulder. "Even so," she said, "you girls are getting practice at listening, focusing, and thinking on your feet!"

Amy nodded. She hadn't thought about it that way.

"And there's a practice round tomorrow," Marion reminded everyone.

All the teams were invited to come to the theater on Saturday. They would have a turn sitting up onstage. The Quiz Bowl host would even ask them a few practice questions.

Amy's mom drove the girls to the theater. They walked in. Amy relaxed a little. There were only about a dozen people there. Some were kids on teams, waiting for their

turn to practice. Some were parents.

*This is good,* Amy thought. *I'll be able to get used to everything without the whole audience here.*

They watched a few teams take their turns onstage. It didn't seem like any big deal. So when it was

the girls' turn, Amy walked right up with her friends.

They walked over to take their seats behind a table that was facing the audience. For the first time, Amy noticed the set of bright lights shining down on the stage. It was hard to see.

Then Amy's vision adjusted. She looked out. She felt every pair of eyes in the room staring at them. All of a sudden, it seemed like so many more people were there!

And look how many seats there were! Sure, they were empty today. But tomorrow they would be filled. Every single one!

Amy estimated how many seats were in the theater. Five hundred? A thousand?

She was so distracted that she didn't even hear the first practice question. Liz nudged her gently.

"Amy?" she said. "Do you know this one?"

Amy jumped a little. The host read it a second time: "The original Nancy Drew mystery series was written by several authors under what pen name?"

Of course Amy knew the answer! Carolyn Keene! Amy had read almost every book in the series. Her heart was racing. Her legs were shaking under the table. But she took a deep breath and she opened her mouth to answer.

No sound came out.

She cleared her throat and tried again. This time, she managed to get the first syllable out. "Car—"

But it was barely a whisper. The host put a hand to his ear. "I'm sorry," he said. "Can you speak up, please?"

Amy's heart was pounding so hard she could hear it in her ears. It felt like the answer was stuck in her throat.

"Are you okay?" Ellie whispered.

Amy felt tears filling her eyes. She stood up and ran off the stage.

# Chapter 7

# A Shady Idea!

Inside the chicken run, Amy tossed cracked corn at the chickens. They squawked and ran in all directions.

"I know how you feel," she said gloomily.

She groaned, remembering that morning. After she'd run off the stage, her friends had come after her. They tried to figure out what

was wrong. But Amy just wanted to go home.

Later she'd talked it over with her mom.

"You don't have to be on the

team," her mom said. "It's okay if you don't want to do it."

"But I *do* want to," Amy replied. "I just don't think I can."

At The Critter Club that day, Amy had decided. She needed to tell the girls that she had to quit.

Marion, Ellie, and Liz arrived a short time later. They hurried over to Amy. "We called your house," Ellie said gently.

"We were worried," Liz added. "Your mom said we'd find you here."

"Are you okay?" Marion asked.

Amy nodded. She took a deep breath. This was it. She had to tell them now.

"Amy," Marion said, before Amy could speak. "We know what the problem is."

Caught off guard, Amy was quiet and listened.

"You know the answers to the questions," Liz said. "You just get nervous!"

Ellie nodded. "I get nervous too, any time I perform."

Amy was shocked to hear that. Ellie? *Nervous?*

"You *never* seem nervous," Amy

said. "So what do you do? How do you get rid of your nerves?"

Ellie shrugged. "Well, I pretend like I'm just performing in my own living room. For my family!"

Amy thought about it. She never felt nervous answering questions with just the girls there. "But the theater is so big!" Amy said. "It's

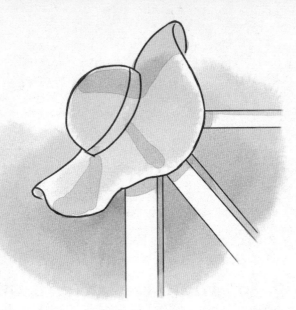

hard to pretend no one's there when so many people *are*."

Amy gazed off into the distance, as if looking out into the audience. She saw something on a fence post by the barn. It was Ms. Sullivan's floppy hat. She'd left it outside again. One time, the girls had tried it on. It was so big on them it came down over their eyes.

*Wait a second,* thought Amy. *What if I really couldn't see the audience? Would it be easier to pretend they weren't there?*

Suddenly Amy ran over and grabbed the hat.

"Guys!" she cried. "I have an idea!"

# Chapter 8

# The Quiz Bowl

"Good afternoon, ladies and gentleman!" the host announced. "Welcome to the Santa Vista Quiz Bowl!"

From backstage, Amy heard the audience erupt into applause. It sure sounded like a full house!

Liz, Ellie, and Marion were at Amy's side. Ellie gave Amy's

hand a squeeze. "Ready?"

Amy nodded. They had spoken to the host earlier. Amy asked if it was okay to wear the floppy hat onstage. "It might help me be less nervous," she explained.

The host gave her a kind smile. "If it works for you, it works for me!" he said.

The girls could hear that the host was about to introduce the second- and third-grade teams. Then they'd go out onstage.

Liz tapped Amy's shoulder. Amy peeked out from under the brim. "Look," Liz said, pointing to a big backstage mirror.

In the reflection, Amy almost didn't recognize herself with the hat on. She giggled. Then she heard

the host announcing the first team.

"Team number one, The Whiz Kids, who are last year's defending champions—Samantha, Danielle, Aiden, and Joseph!"

The audience applauded again. Marion took Amy's hand. "I think we're next!"

"Team number two, The Critter Club Girls!" said the host. "Ellie, Marion, Amy, and Liz!"

Marion led Amy out onstage. Amy tried to ignore the applause. She kept her head down as they took their seats at their table. She listened and clapped for the other teams.

BOWL

Teams three and four were second-grade teams. Team five was a mixed team with two second graders and two third graders.

"Good luck to all the teams!" said the host. "And now a quick review of the rules."

Each team had a buzzer. Whoever buzzed in first could answer. If they answered correctly, their team got a point. If not, another team could buzz in and answer. "The team with the most points at the end of the round is our winner!"

Amy took a deep breath. So far,

the hat was working! In her head she knew that there was a huge audience watching her. *And they're probably wondering what's up with the hat,* Amy thought.

But without seeing them, Amy could almost imagine they weren't there. Her body felt calm.

The host cleared his throat. "Here is the first question. What term describes two words or phrases that mean the same thing?"

Amy knew they'd learned this in language arts. But she couldn't think of the word. She and the girls

huddled up to talk it over.

"Is it 'thesaurus'?" Liz asked.

Amy shook her head. She knew that wasn't it.

*BUZZZZZZZZZ!* Another team

buzzed in. "Team one, do you have an answer?" the host asked.

"Synonym!" said Samantha, loud and clear.

Right away, Amy knew it was right. Team one got the first point.

The audience applauded. Then the host was on to the next question. "What are the four stages of a butterfly's life cycle?"

Four words flashed through

Amy's mind as bright as a neon sign. She knew it! She was sure!

Amy reached out for the buzzer.

Then she froze. If she pushed it, everyone in the whole theater would look at her.

But if she didn't, one of the other teams might get their point!

*BUZZZZZZZ!*

"Team two," Amy heard the host say. "Do you have an answer?"

# Chapter 9

# And the Winner Is . . .

The whole theater was silent. Everyone was waiting for Amy to answer. She opened her mouth—

But her mind was a blank! The answer was gone!

Then Amy heard a voice in her ear. "Take a breath," Marion whispered.

"Team two, I need an answer,"

the host said. "What are the four stages of a butterfly's life cycle?"

Amy smiled. She breathed. The answer came flooding back. "Egg, caterpillar, chrysalis, and butterfly," Amy said. Her voice sounded louder than she'd expected.

There was a pause. Then the host said, "That is correct!"

The whole theater clapped. Amy could even hear a couple of cheers. Amy couldn't help but smile.

Suddenly she felt an urge to take a peek.

She looked out from under the

brim of her hat. Yep. There were a *lot* of people there. And everyone *was* looking at her.

But somehow it didn't feel like such a big deal. It just looked like a room of people who wanted all the teams to do well.

Amy took off the hat. She tucked it safely under her seat. She glanced over at her teammates. Their smiles and thumbs-up made Amy smile even wider.

The next half hour was a blur. Amy's team knew lots of answers! But so did team one, The Whiz Kids.

The host held up a question card. "We have come to the end of

the round. I have one question left. Two teams are tied for the lead— team one and team two. I would like to use this last question as our tiebreaker. Only teams one and two may buzz in. Are we ready?"

Amy wasn't sure she was ready. But she tried to focus on the question. Whoever got the answer right would win!

The host read: "What is a group of lions called?"

Amy almost jumped out of her seat. She knew it! She reached for the buzzer.

*BUZZZZZZ!*

The other team had buzzed in first!

"Team one, do you have an answer?" the host asked.

"Yes," Danielle said calmly. "It's a herd."

The crowd was silent, waiting for the host's reply.

"I'm sorry," the host said gently. "That is not correct."

Immediately Amy hit her team's buzzer. She felt everyone looking at her again. But she didn't care!

Without waiting for the host to ask her, Amy called out the answer.

"It's a pride!" she said. "A pride of lions."

The host smiled at her. "That *is* correct . . . and we have a winner! Team number two, The Critter Club Girls! Congratulations!"

The audience clapped louder than ever. Amy looked at her friends. They were shrieking with delight! Then they were around her, hugging her from all sides.

Amy laughed and cheered—for her team and for herself.

# Chapter 10

# What Do You Call a Little Chicken?

The next day after school, Ms. Sullivan baked a cake to celebrate. On her back patio, the girls sat around the table. Ms. Sullivan cut the cake and passed out slices.

"I can't believe we won!" Ellie exclaimed.

"And beat a team of third graders!" Marion added.

"Well, I am extremely proud of all of you," Ms. Sullivan said. "It was a big challenge—in lots of ways." She gave Amy a wink.

Amy smiled. "It was even kind of . . . *fun!*" she admitted. She was so glad she hadn't quit. She wasn't sure she'd ever love being onstage. But she knew she could do it.

Later, a pickup truck drove up the gravel driveway. "Oh!" said Ms. Sullivan. "It's Mr. Taylor. He's here to pick up the chickens."

They went out front to meet him. Then they showed him to the chicken coop.

"Wow, what a coop!" Mr. Taylor

said, admiring their work.

The girls explained that the neighbors had built it. "But we painted it!" Liz said proudly.

"Well," said Mr. Taylor, "I should have you girls come paint *my* chicken coop!"

He leaned down and peeked inside. Then he looked up at the girls. "Well, well, well," he said. "Do you hear that?"

The girls peeked into the coop too. Amy could hear a faint *peep, peep, peep.* She looked more closely at the nesting boxes. All three hens

were sitting on a clutch of eggs. And there was one tiny chick in each box! They looked like they had just hatched!

"They're soooooo cute," Ellie cooed.

"You know," Mr. Taylor said, "it

usually takes twenty-one days for chicken eggs to hatch."

Amy did some quick math. Twenty-one days was three weeks. And the chickens had come to The Critter Club almost exactly three weeks ago. That meant they had laid the eggs as soon as they'd arrived!

*Wow,* Amy thought. *A lot has happened in the last three weeks! Some of it in the Quiz Bowl. And some of it in the chicken coop!*

If you like the Critter Club, you'll also enjoy
# The Adventures of Sophie Mouse!

*Buzz, buzz, buzzzzzzz.* Outside the Mouse family's cottage, a bumblebee zipped from flower to flower.

Sitting at her easel in the sunshine, Sophie Mouse put down her paintbrush. Her eyes followed the bee. *Oh, to be able to fly,* she thought. *I could see every inch of Silverlake Forest—maybe even to the*

*other side of Forget-Me-Not Lake! I*
*wonder how fast a bee flies when he*
*really gets going. What would it be*
*like to fly to the schoolhouse for the*
*first day of school tomorrow? What*
*would—*

"Sophie? Sophie!" Her father's voice called out, snapping her out of her daydream. He was in the doorway of their cottage, which was nestled in between the roots of an oak tree. "Are you done with your chores?" George Mouse asked. "When you are, you can go see Mom at the bakery. She's making nutmeg popovers today!"

Sophie's little nose twitched. She was sure she could already smell the sweet scent. Nutmeg popovers were one of her mother's specialties. At her bakery in Pine Needle Grove, Lily Mouse surely would have started making the batter at dawn, before Sophie was even awake.

Sophie hated to stop painting. It was the first spring day warm enough to paint outside! But she had a little sweeping to do if she wanted to go to the bakery.

Sophie hurried inside and found

the willow-twig broom. She had already swept the three small bedrooms upstairs. Just the main floor was left: under the toadstool table and birch-branch stools, and around the spun-silk couch. Sophie swept all the corners of the kitchen. Then she swept the pile of leaf bits and dust right out the front door.

"Dad! I'm finished!" she called. "I'm going by Hattie's house on the way to the bakery!"

# the CRITTER club

## Join the club!

31901056510532